Pickles
Sniffs it Out

This story is based on a real incident - and on a real dog, called Pickles. This is the story of how Pickles became front page news.

Michaela Morgan and Dee Shulman

Collins

Look out for more *Jumbo Jets* from Collins

Finlay MacTrebble and the Fantastic Fertiliser • **Scoular Anderson**

Forecast of Fear • **Keith Brumpton**

Trouble on the Day • **Norma Clarke**

The Curse of Brian's Brick • **James Andrew Hall**

Invasion of the Dinner Ladies • **Michaela Morgan**

We Won the Lottery • **Shoo Rayner**

Bernie Works a Miracle • **Leon Rosselson**

Charlie and Biff • *Fergus the Forgetful* • *Fidgety Felix* •
Queen Lizzie Rules OK • **Margaret Ryan**

My Mum • **Dee Shulman**

The Man in Shades • *Talking Pictures* • **Pat Thomson**

Sir Quinton Quest Hunts the Yeti •
Sir Quinton Quest Hunts the Jewel • **Kay Umansky**

Gosh Look Teddy, it's a Werewolf • **Bob Wilson**

The Baked Bean Cure • *Dad's Dodgy Lodger* • **Philip Wooderson**

To Lucas, who taught me all I know about dogs

First published by A & C Black Ltd in 1994
Published by Collins in 1994
10 9 8 7 6 5 4
Collins is an imprint of HarperCollins*Publishers* Ltd,
77–85 Fulham Palace Road, Hammersmith, London W6 8JB

ISBN 0 00 674810-4

Text © Michaela Morgan 1994
Illustrations © Dee Shulman 1994

The author and the illustrator assert the moral right to
be identified as the author and the illustrator of the work.
A CIP record for this title is available from the British Library.
Printed and bound in Great Britain by
Caledonian International Book Manufacturing Ltd, Glasgow

CHAPTER ONE

It's a dog's life

Smells! Don't you just love them? I do!
I love the smells of the street and people's
feet, cheese, fresh air and underwear.
Not to mention steak and chops – and
yesterday's socks. But most of all I love
the meaty, crunchy smells of BONES.

Bones are the best!

I love to sniff them out.

sniff

sniff

I love to CRUNCH them up

I love to bury them.

PAT

PAT

and I love to dig them up again!

Strangely enough, my people aren't so keen. They really don't have a lot of sense. When they see me with a really impressive huge, ripe, smelly bone you might expect them to say

but what they do say is

and before I can even bark, another bone hits the bin. It's a dog's life!

CHAPTER TWO

A shaggy dog and his story

Humans can be loyal and lovable but they are very difficult to train.

My people can understand simple commands like

and

but they don't really understand me.

Take this one for instance. He's one of my people. They call him John. He has the usual schoolboy smells

gravy

inky fingers

well-picked scab

soggy socks

muddy shoes

and all he says is

Go away Pickles!

Not now Pickles!

WOOF!

WOOF!

'Clear off Pickles!' He says I'm not a 'real' dog because I'm not the fast and fierce type. He thinks I'm just a dull and dozy, lying around sort of dog.

Little does he know!

The other one is just staying here for a while. This one is called Frankie. Frankie is a girl. Surprised? So was John. He had been sent a few postcards from his new penfriend in America. They said things like

and one day

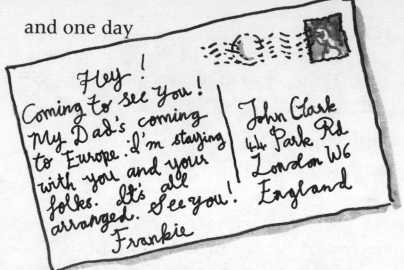

Hey!
Coming to see you!
My Dad's coming
to Europe. I'm staying
with you and your
folks. It's all
arranged. See you!
Frankie

John Clark
44 Park Rd
London W6
England

At about the same time John's dad and mum got a letter from Frankie's dad.

Mr Chuck Tolliver
523 Tamarind Street
San Francisco CA 99 4107

Dear Mr and Mrs Clark,

I have to come to Europe on urgent business. As our kids are penfriends I thought this would be a good opportunity for them to meet. Perhaps Frankie could stay with you for a while? Time is very short. I'm setting out immediately so I suggest we just call on you to discuss arrangements when we get to London,

Yours sincerely,

Chuck Tolliver

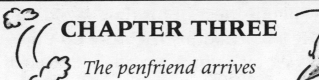

CHAPTER THREE

The penfriend arrives

John could hardly wait to show this penfriend off to all his gang.

Imagine the scene when 'he' turned out to be 'she'.

John spends most of his time avoiding her. He's worried his friends won't be impressed by a girl – a really tall, freckly girl, with a mouth full of metal and a grumpy look. He's so fed up he even talks to ME about it all. He says

she's bossy...

...she's big-headed...

...and she boasts!

It's true.

She calls it soccer and she calls it BORING. She calls John 'Johnnie'. He hates it.

But I like her. She wears nice soft shoes, chewy and rubbery. She smells of sunshine and open air. She calls me 'cute' and she tickles my ears.

They both complain

13

His mother sighs

he protests.

'I've let her look at my football cards, haven't I? I said she could watch my football practice didn't I? And today I'm taking her to the BIGGEST and BEST stamp exhibition ever – with a chance to see the WORLD CUP! You'd think she'd be over the moon wouldn't you? But what did she say? She said:

She's BORING!'

These two kids may not have a lot in common but I'll say this for them – they can both read.

This can come in handy at times.

To tell you the truth, I'm no great reader but even I was getting the hang of this sign.

'We can't take him all the way home again,' moaned John.

'Leave 'im here,' suggested the guard at the door. 'Tie him up. I'll keep an eye on him.'

'I'll tie him,' Frankie said. 'I know all about knots.'

'You would,' muttered John.

'This is a special knot. The sort only scouts, soldiers and famous explorers can do. I learned it at camp. Let's see . . .

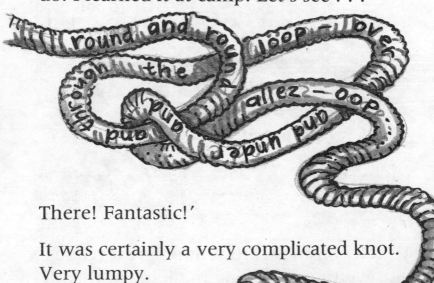

round and round loop over through the pud pud allez—oop pud under pud

There! Fantastic!'

It was certainly a very complicated knot. Very lumpy.

And it was fantastic.

Fantastically unsuccessful. It fell apart as soon as I sneezed.

I barked helpfully, to let the guard know, but he was too busy to notice.

So, inspired by all the talk of scouts and explorers, I thought I'd do a little bit of exploring of my own.

CHAPTER FIVE

I decided to have a sniff around the back of the building. These areas can be treasure troves of trash – rich in rubbish of the smelly, tasty variety. While I was busy grubbing about there, a very interesting smell went by. I caught a glimpse of a sack being carried into the building. More importantly I caught a wonderful whiff of meat – and bone.
'Follow that bone!'
I said to myself and I was off.

In through a back door—

—along a corridor—

—up some stairs.

Nose to the ground like a real tracker dog.
I had no trouble following that beefy trail
but it was beginning to get mixed up with
the scent of the man and the sack. There
was the rich aroma of sock —
wet and woolly and
slightly stale. This was
mixed with an
appealing blend of shoe and
trouser and hair oil —
all past their first flush of
freshness. It was the smell
of a man who, like me, keeps
a respectful distance from
soap and water. A powerful pong —
perfect to trail.

But what was this? Another smell
creeping up. The unmistakable smell of
. . . another dog . . . another BIG dog . . .
another big, fierce dog. A guard dog, all
teeth and tonsils.

This dog raised his head
and glared. He rose to his
feet and stood there looking
every inch the winner of
the Guard Dog of the Year
contest. He snarled.
He bared his teeth and growled.

Help!

But the dog wasn't looking at me. He was looking at the man. And here's the sad part of the story. The man reached into his sack and pulled out a lovely gloppy handful of raw meat. Then he pulled out more meat and a bone – a GIGANTIC bone. Before my drooling lips he tossed them all to Mr Guard Dog of the Year – every single scrap.

The guard dog went into reverse. He stopped growling. He tucked his teeth back inside his mouth. He backed away from the man, sank back down on the floor and got down to the important business of chewing and crunching a really wonderful bone.

The man sneaked by.

Unless you're a dog (and if you're reading this then you're probably not) you will find it difficult to fully understand my disappointment. I'd smelled a perfect bone. I'd seen a perfect bone. But I hadn't had so much as a lick of it.

My only hope was that this man had another little scrap left in a corner of his sack – just a snack, a tiny titbit that he might toss my way. With this in mind I carried on trailing him.

CHAPTER SIX

Adventure

The man with the sack set off down another empty corridor. I was close behind, following his trail and sniffing the cold corridor smells of dust and disinfectant.

I caught sight of the man running up some concrete steps and I slunk, almost invisible in the shadows, behind him.

I got to the top just in time to see him reach into his sack and pull something out.

But, sadly, it wasn't a bone, it was just a big metal bar. He glanced around, then gripped the bar tightly and pushed it against the lock. He put all his weight behind it and forced the door open.

He slid inside, sneaky as a cat. I slipped in behind him.

The exhibition hall was a brightly lit,
crowded room. It smelled of warm
raincoats and hummed with the sound of
humans talking. Among the crowd I
could see Frankie and John.

With a group of people and a tour guide, they were peering into a glass case.

'I'll be in trouble if they find me here,' I thought. So like a sausage dog, I laid low.

The man stuffed his sack into his coat, and pretended to be one of the crowd. I stayed in the shadows.

Solid gold! WOW!

John had his nose pressed up against the glass.

I guess it's worth a lot.

Frankie looked almost interested.

The kids caught up with their group and moved on to another room in the exhibition. The next group had not yet arrived. The room was quiet and empty.

Quick as a flash, the man slipped out of the shadows.

He darted up to the display case. With one quick movement he prised the padlock off the back of the display case slid his hand in and grabbed the gold cup. He stuffed it in his sack and then he was back through the door. Fast as a whippet, he disappeared leaving me alone and puzzled in the exhibition hall.

CHAPTER SEVEN

Doggone!

Don't ask me what happened. How should I know? I'm a dog. But one thing I DO know is that whenever something gets smashed or taken or eaten, whenever there's a mysterious crash or an unexplained smell, all the humans look round for the nearest dog and blame him. So, as the nearest dog, I decided to scarper.

Back down the stairs -

-Along the corridor -

-through the back door.

On the way back I had a bit of luck. Mr Fierce Bad Guard Dog of the Year had turned into Mr Snoozy Woozy Dog of the Year.

29

Yep. He was just lying there looking dazed and dozy and snoring gently.

Brave as a bulldog, I snatched his bone and ran off.

In less than two shakes of a dog's tail I was back outside the building, lying exactly where those kids had left me – and just about to sink my teeth into one beautiful ripe bone when . . .

And off I went, dragged along on my lead.

Lucky Pickles didn't wander off when he slipped his leash.

He wouldn't do that, he's not the adventurous type.

He thinks all I ever do is snooze on the sofa and refuse to do tricks. He doesn't realize I can hear, smell, and sense things he knows nothing about.

At this very moment, for instance, I can sense waves of panic and anxiety growing behind us. Small groups of guards are gathering. I can hear them whispering. Doors are being locked, people are being stopped and a worried looking woman is picking up the phone and dialling 999.

'Emergency. Which service do you require?' asks the operator.

CHAPTER EIGHT

Read all about it!

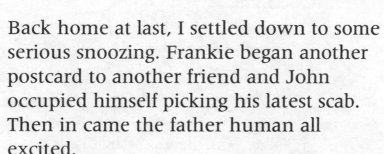

Back home at last, I settled down to some serious snoozing. Frankie began another postcard to another friend and John occupied himself picking his latest scab. Then in came the father human all excited.

Well! You kids have certainly had your share of excitement today, eh! Who would have believed it? Daylight robbery!

Both kids looked even blanker than usual
– until they noticed the newspaper
headline.

'Oh no!' said John 'Does this mean the
tournament will be cancelled?'

'Oh wow!' said Frankie. 'We were there!
We're witnesses!' And she marched off to
the phone. 'Put me through to Scotland
Yard,' she said importantly.

CHAPTER NINE

The thin-lipped man

So Frankie and John were interviewed
and gave the police full details of
everything they as intelligent, alert,
sensitive humans had seen and heard and
noticed.

Nobody bothered to ask me, of course. But I could really have told them a thing or two.

The policeman did say something interesting though. Apparently, several other people had noticed a 'suspicious character' and the police had put together a description of him.

HAVE YOU SEEN THIS MAN?

• LATE 30's 5'10", SLIM
• DARK HAIR GREASED BACK
• THIN LIPS

We started to see posters everywhere.

On walls.

On buses.

On telly.

This poster also started to appear

and as the days went by without news the reward got bigger and bigger.

CHAPTER TEN

The hunt is on

John was fed up. 'It could all be cancelled now. No World Cup. It's a disaster . . .' he sighed.

But Frankie was excited. She was determined to solve the mystery. No man even remotely fitting the description was safe from her suspicions.

We wandered up and down streets, peering into people's faces and guessing at the width of their lips.

But it never quite worked out.

I didn't say anything. I'm a dog, remember – but I did whine a bit just to show willing.

CHAPTER ELEVEN

Fed up

So now both kids were fed up.

'Come on you two,' said the mother human, 'it's not the end of the world.'

But it was the end of the world for John. He, and millions of other football fans listened to every radio announcement, watched every TV feature and read every newspaper, desperate to hear that the cup had been found. But day after day, the news was the same

I know what it's like to search for something that always seems to get away. I hadn't had so much as a sniff of a bone for days. I knew exactly how fed up the football fans felt.

Frankie had been quiet since the police told her to leave the detecting to them. All three of us felt that life was just one long grey wet weekend.

announced the mum.

'What you all need is a good brisk walk in the fresh air,' said the poor deluded parent. 'Hurry up before it gets too dark.'

Whoever said humans were intelligent?

John was dragging his feet. Frankie was dragging me. This wasn't a 'nice brisk walk'. It was a drag.

The only sound was the squeak of John's shoes, the odd sigh from the forlorn Frankie, and my sniffs.

Sniffing is the nicest bit about walks. Interesting smells tonight included the friendly smell of a popular lamp post, the wet and leafy smell of hedges, the cool of the night air and . . . something else, a sort of oily smell strangely familiar and getting closer.

Then my poor highly sensitive ears were blasted by the piercing sound of a police whistle. Another whistle shrieked out, and then sounds of shouting and clumping feet racing along the pavement towards us and past us. The man – the one with the hair oil and the sack – the one I'd trailed – pushed past us. Some distance behind him panted two blue-suited policemen shouting

STOP THAT MAN!

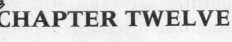

'It's HIM!' yelled Frankie. 'The thin lipped man!' and she was off after him.

Careful Frankie. He could be dangerous!

For a human, Frankie is a great runner. She's nothing compared to a greyhound, you understand. But compared to the policeman, John, and even me, she is fast.

She fairly pounded along the pavement getting closer and closer to him. We puffed along behind, near enough to see her launch herself at the man. With a magnificent Karate-type call she jumped on him and caught hold of his coat. 'Got you!' she yelled but she spoke too soon.

44

The man thrashed about, struggled, and got away, throwing the coat and Frankie sideways into a hedge.

She ed.

Whether she was howling in anger, frustration, or because the hedge was the thorny kind, I don't know. This I do know. It was LOUD. Ear splittingly loud. But not so loud that my supersensitive ears didn't pick up the noise of something else falling. My nose started twitching too.

 I thought.

John let go of my lead and helped Frankie up.

'I'm OK,' she said. 'Come on!' and they were off again, leaving the pavement now and smashing through gardens, leaping through hedges, clattering over dustbins with the police shouting at them, and Frankie shouting at me, 'Get him Pickles! PICKLES! COME ON!'

Obediently, I tagged along. 'This way! It's quicker,' yelled John and we scrambled through another hedge. But the man was drawing further and further away.

'He's getting away,' moaned John.

'Grab a trash can,' panted Frankie, 'roll it at him'.

And that's what they did.

They grabbed dustbins and lids.

They took careful aim, rolled them and bowled them and . . .

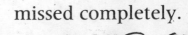

missed completely.

'Oh no!' groaned John. But the commotion had distracted the thin-lipped man. He turned, then stumbled a little, and seemed about to lose his footing. The two policemen speeded up and lunged at him.

'It is my duty to inform you,' panted the first, 'that you are under arrest and anything you say may be taken down and used in evidence against you.'

That man didn't give in easily. He kicked. He fought. He wriggled like a dog being forced into a bath.

But actually I was feeling very hopeful.
Very hopeful indeed!

CHAPTER THIRTEEN

Home again

I was back at home, hiding in my quiet corner of the kitchen when Frankie and John turned up.

Where have you been? Pickles has been back for-oh...

She suddenly noticed the policeman standing behind the kids.

'Not an accident I hope!'

No need to worry Madam - -no bones broken Just a couple of bruises and a bit of...

MUD! shrieked the mother, staring at John. 'Potato peelings! Eggshells!' and then she caught sight of Frankie who was looking, if anything, slightly worse.

What on earth?

I gave them a friendly sniff. They smelt WONDERFUL! Mmmm chicken bones, bits of beefburger, gravy . . . They looked like a dog's dinner.

It's OK – we're fine – and we caught the thin-lipped man!

'Well . . . we helped,' said John, 'a bit'.

'These two children have been getting in our way again,' said the officer, 'interfering in police business. Still . . .' He looked at their tired and dirty faces. 'No harm done – in fact they did slow the man down so we could catch him'.

said the father human. Up to this point he'd just been standing there with his mouth open.

'So the World Cup is back safe and sound! Found by my boy – and his friend, of course.'

'Unfortunately not, sir. We've arrested the man in question but . . .'

'But he didn't have the cup on him,' Frankie interrupted.

'And he won't say where it is . . .' said John.

'And the police have looked everywhere . . .'

'And we've looked too . . .'

'So no reward for us,' sighed Frankie.

With this both kids sank on to the sofa, tired out and fed up.

Hearing dogs mentioned, I lay low. I had a wonderful secret and I didn't want any interfering humans sticking their noses into it.

CHAPTER FOURTEEN

My perfect bone

'Did you say Pickles was back here?' said Frankie.

some dog!

said John. 'He had the chance of catching a crook. A real dog – a bright dog – a brave dog – would stick with a trail but what does Pickles do? Heads off in completely the wrong direction and gets lost!'

'Aw. Poor Pickles,' said Frankie, tickling my ears. 'He tries his best . . .'

What is he doing?

I was lying by the back door. If you lie very flat (and you're a dog) you can sniff the outside air sneaking in through the crack under the door. I could just catch faint whiffs of the garden, the hedge . . . and my treasure. 'Let me at it!' I thought.

'I'll be off now,' said the officer. 'If you think of anything, you know where to find me.' He put on his helmet and went to the door.

Door open. Ready for take off.

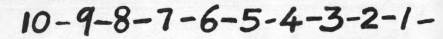

10 – 9 – 8 – 7 – 6 – 5 – 4 – 3 – 2 – 1 –

LAUNCH DOG!

I was off into the garden through the hedge and heading towards my perfect bone.

'You should keep that animal under control,' added the policeman.

But what did I care? I had the wind in my ears, the breeze in my nose, and I was back on the trail, snuffling under hedges, rooting in the leaves for my buried treasure. At last! My perfect bone!

I trotted back proudly, my head held high. This was no easy task. The bone I was carrying was tooth-wrenchingly heavy. It was magnificent — or it would be as soon as I could get it out of the sack.

I'd tracked it down brilliantly, but it was a heavy sort of bone and I was dog-tired. So I'd left it carefully hidden at the end of the garden. Then I got to thinking that some other dog might get a whiff of my bone and steal it away, so I decided to bring it closer to the house where I could keep a better guard on it.

The problem, as always, was my humans. They were looking decidedly unimpressed by my find. They don't have my highly developed tastes.

oh Yuck!

Drop it Pickles! Leave it!

John gingerly took the sack from me. It was very soggy and muddy by now and he wrinkled his nose in disgust and held it at arm's length. 'Dirty old thing,' he said and tossed it to one side.

CLANG!

went the 'dirty old thing'.

noisy sort of bone—

I thought.

John went over to it and prodded it with his toe.

Funny.... Do you think...

Before he could finish, Frankie and the policeman were on it and into it. Then it was all shriekings and skippings, and clapping and whooping, and smirking and smiling. From out of the sack, they brought a large shiny golden cup.

Who's a disappointed doggy then? I wanted to snarl because I have to tell you that I've searched every inch of that sack now, inside and out, and there isn't a hint of a bone there. There's just the scent of a long gone bone and a huge gold cup that isn't meaty or chewy at all.

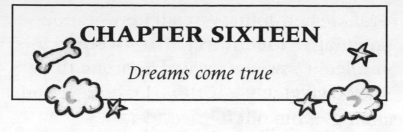

CHAPTER SIXTEEN

Dreams come true

You wouldn't believe the fuss that was made during the next few days — newspapers, radio, television.

Frankie sent off stacks of postcards.

And then there was the presentation. This was what the humans call a 'big day'. Inevitably, a 'big day' involves a lot of humans running around in panic and stepping on your paws, so you can understand I wasn't too keen.

Frankie and John were all new-smelling in their finery. They were thrilled. I was less excited. For one thing they'd given me a bath . . .

UGH!

and a brushing . . .

OUCH!

and . . . a ribbon.

I just hope I don't meet any of my pals.

There wasn't much chance of that as we were all put into a huge black car. We were driven to a big building with lots of people and lights.

I sat dutifully while all the humans yattered and chattered.

Then it was the high spot of the evening – the presentation. The kids were given three medium-sized pieces of paper,

two small pieces of paper

and one very small piece of paper.

Everyone was clapping and
cheering, and Frankie and John
were bowing and smiling. Me?
I couldn't see the point of all
these pieces of paper. They
weren't even being used to
wrap something up.

'And now a very special
reward,' said the
announcer, 'for a
very special
little dog'.

The humans were standing and stamping, whooping and yelling. They talk of 'mad dogs' but I can tell you, I was the most sensible creature in the room as I sat there quietly waiting for my 'special reward' – no doubt ANOTHER piece of paper. But what did I see?

An enormous, ripe, crunchy, stupendous, tremendous, PERFECT bone!

I couldn't help it, I had to join in with the general madness. I was jumping and grinning and yapping and licking and the crowd were clapping, and clapping and clapping.

CLAP!

This is the best day of my life.

CLAP

I thought.

'The day I finally found my perfect bone. The day my dreams came true.'

On July 30th, 1966 the World Cup final was played at Wembley Stadium. Around the rest of the world, 40 million people tuned in and held their breath as the two teams, England and West Germany, battled it out. It was a tough match. It was a thrilling match. The final score, 4:2 to England!

A huge cheer went up as the Queen presented the famous cup to the home team. Cheering, clapping, chanting, yelling, the crowd went wild as the famous cup was held high and paraded around the stadium in triumph.

And back at home in front of the telly one small dog gave a contented woof as he lay and snoozed next to his enormous, his precious, his PERFECT bone.